Twin Trouble

backpack Mysteries

9701

a backpack Mystery

Twin Trouble

Mary Carpenter Reid

BETHANY HOUSE PUBLISHERS
MINNEAPOLIS, MINNESOTA 55438

Twin Trouble
Copyright © 1997
Mary Carpenter Reid

Cover and story illustrations by Paul Turnbaugh

Published by Bethany House Publishers
A Ministry of Bethany Fellowship, Inc.
11300 Hampshire Avenue South
Minneapolis, Minnesota 55438

Printed in the United States of America.

Library of Congress Cataloging-in-Publication Data

Reid, Mary.
    Twin trouble / by Mary Carpenter Reid.
        p.   cm. — (A Backpack mystery ; 4)
    Summary: While visiting their consins Belinda and Melinda, who work at a camping resort and tell people about Jesus, Steff and her younger sister Paulie investigate a theft and other suspicious occurrences.
    ISBN 1–55661–718–6
    [1. Cousins—Fiction. 2. Christian life—Fiction. 3. Mystery and detective stories.] I. Title. II. Series: Reid, Mary. Backpack mystery ; 4.
PZ7.R2727Tw   1996
[Fic]—dc21   97–4650
                                                    CIP
                                                     AC

To Jo Caroline—
my very own sister.

MARY CARPENTER REID loves to visit places just like the places Steff and Paulie visit. Does she stay with peculiar relatives? That's her secret!

She will tell you her family is wonderful. She likes reading and writing children's books. She like colors and computers. She especially likes getting letters from her readers.

She can't organize things as well as Steff does, but she makes lots of lists.

Two cats—a calico and a tiger cat—live at her house in California. *They* are very peculiar!

contents

Whatever you do, work at it with all your heart, as working for the Lord.

Colossians 3:23

oNe red eye

"What was that?" Steff Larson twisted in the backseat of the car. "We passed something red and shiny."

"Where?" asked her younger sister, Paulie.

"On my side. It was glowing in the dark."

"How big was it?" asked Paulie.

"Tiny."

"How tiny?"

"Never mind. It's way behind us now," said Steff.

The car swooped along the mountain road.

Its headlight beams raced over trunks of giant sequoia trees.

The driver hit the brakes for a curve.

Steff and Paulie flew against their seat belts.

"Belinda!" scolded the woman beside the driver.

"Oops!" said Belinda. "Sorry, Melinda. Sorry, girls."

Paulie asked Steff, "Was it tiny like a red ruby ring?"

Melinda turned to the backseat. "Perhaps Steff saw an animal in the woods, or a faraway campfire."

Steff said, "I suppose it could have been an animal—if it was a really tall animal with one eye—a red eye."

"Weird!" said Paulie. "I'd rather see a ruby ring."

Belinda and Melinda laughed.

Steff tried to laugh, too. It wasn't easy. Being here on this dark road gave her a lonely feeling, even though she and Paulie were with their father's twin cousins.

Every summer, Belinda and Melinda lived

at the Grumlet Giant Trees Resort and ran the Grumlet Giant Trees Store.

The twins laughed a lot and wore pretty clothes. They didn't act old like some adults did.

Steff thought staying with them might be fun—partly because the resort had a stable.

"Are you sure Paulie and I can ride horses?" she asked.

"Of course," said Belinda.

Melinda warned, "Don't let the two trail hands at the stable scare you away. Ned and Zachery sometimes get crabby."

"We call them the Grumlet Grumps." Belinda giggled. "But don't tell anyone."

Paulie said, "I'm not afraid of any old Grumlet Grumps."

Belinda turned the car sharply. "Grumlet Giant Trees Resort coming up!"

Paulie's backpack slid across the seat.

They drove down a narrow road. Sequoia tree trunks crowded close.

One was big enough to drive the car through—if there had been a hole.

"That must be the biggest tree in the world!" cried Paulie.

"One of the biggest," said Melinda. "And one of the oldest."

Belinda said, "Some sequoia trees have been growing since before Jesus was born."

"Two thousand years!" exclaimed Steff.

Paulie said, "That's two thousand birthdays!"

Steff wished her mother and father could see these trees. But they had gone to a businees meeting.

Her father had told Steff and Paulie, "This meeting is important to our family business. Remember, the family business makes the money we use to pay our bills."

The car stopped in a dirt parking lot.

"We're here!" Belinda said. She turned off the lights.

"This is a very dark resort," said Paulie.

"Oh!" groaned Melinda. "The electricity is off again."

"I have to iron something to wear tomorrow," said Belinda.

"I need to polish my toenails," said Melinda. "How can I do that in the dark?"

"The question is—how can we get to the cabin in the dark?" said Belinda. "Did you bring a flashlight?"

"Me?"

Steff opened her backpack. "I have a flashlight."

"Oh, you're wonderful!" said Belinda.

"I do, too." Paulie pulled a flashlight from her backpack.

Paulie's batteries were dead.

So, the four of them carried the suitcases and followed the spot of light Steff shone on the ground.

The path went between trees and around dark buildings.

"Our store is over there," said Belinda. "Grumlet Giant Trees Store. You'll love it."

"All except the smelly fish bait," said Melinda.

"Ugh!" said Paulie.

"Ugh!" said Steff.

Melinda grabbed Steff's arm. "Stop!" She

pointed to a small moving light and said, "Belinda, could someone be in our store?"

"I certainly hope not."

"You know the problem we've been having. . . ."

Belinda quickly said, "Talk about that later. There, the light is gone."

They walked on.

"Here's our cabin!" Melinda said.

They stood on the path, loaded with Steff's and Paulie's suitcases.

Steff shone her flashlight up the cabin steps to the porch. She said, "I'll hold the light. Somebody can open the door. Then we'll carry the stuff inside."

"My, you are organized," said Belinda.

"Steff is always organized," Paulie told her.

Just then, the electricity came back on.

Later, Steff and Paulie sat on the beds in their room.

Steff turned off the light. "Say your prayers," she told her sister.

Steff started to push aside the curtain and look out the window. Instead, she flopped down and covered up. She didn't want to see another red eye.

She said a special prayer about whatever problem the cousins were having at the store.

Belinda and Melinda had not wanted to talk about something. Maybe they thought it would frighten Steff and Paulie.

It did kind of frighten Steff.

2

pink opens the store

The next morning, Steff and Paulie found a note from the twins and a map of the resort.

Go to the dining hall. We'll meet you there.

A boy stood at the door to the dining hall.

"Hi! I'm Chet. You can go in. Your cousins will be here soon."

"How do you know about our cousins?" asked Steff.

"I work here."

He seemed only a little older than Steff.

She said, "Sure you do."

Several long tables held food for breakfast. The girls took waffles and strawberries.

The twins came into the dining hall carrying Bibles.

Steff wished she had an outfit like the pretty one Melinda wore.

"Oooh, waffles," said Melinda.

Belinda licked her lips. "And strawberries."

As they ate, Belinda said, "We have Bible study most mornings."

"You girls can come tomorrow if you want," said Melinda.

"Okay," Steff said. "Does that boy at the door work here?"

"Chet? Sort of," Melinda said. "His father runs the dining hall."

A woman stopped by the table. She asked the twins, "Are you having Bible story hour for the children again this year?"

"Oh yes," said Belinda.

"Good. My children want to come."

Steff said, "Mom and Dad didn't say this was a Christian resort."

Belinda smiled. "It isn't."

"But," said Melinda, "Mr. Grumlet is happy for us to tell Bible stories."

"And have Bible studies," added Belinda.

"And help Pastor Harl Sunday mornings."

"Many people who come here don't know anything about the Lord," said Belinda.

"That's why we work at the store every summer," said Melinda.

"Yes." Belinda nodded. "The rest of the year, we decorate houses for people—you know, help them choose wallpaper and . . ."

"Rugs and curtains. But we never take decorating jobs during the summer. . . ."

"So we can come up here. . . ."

"And tell people about Jesus."

Belinda leaned forward and said softly, "You see, it's kind of our ministry."

Melinda nodded. "We call it our Little Ministry in the Big Trees."

Steff blinked. Listening to the twins talk was like listening to a tennis game. Back and forth—back and forth.

Across the room, a boy in a wheelchair sat

at a table. A woman was helping him eat. They were spilling a lot. Red strawberry juice dribbled down the boy's chin.

Melinda stood up. "I think Mrs. Smith could use a break."

She took the woman's place and began helping the boy eat his breakfast.

Steff watched. Melinda kept talking and smiling, no matter how much food got on the boy and the floor, and on her pretty outfit.

Steff didn't know if she could smile at a boy who was drooling red strawberry juice.

After breakfast, the girls walked with Belinda and Melinda to the Grumlet Giant Trees Store.

Belinda held up a key. The round end was covered with pink plastic.

She sang, "Pink opens the door to our store—and our storeroom."

"To be correct," said Melinda. "Mr. Grumlet owns the store. But . . ."

"We manage it for him."

Melinda pointed to a building behind the store. "That's the storeroom."

"We spent two days cleaning it," said Belinda.

"To make room for a big shipment of camping equipment that will be delivered Monday. Mostly tents."

"Yes, a hiking club ordered the very best." Belinda rolled her eyes. "It cost thousands of dollars."

"The club will camp on the trail for weeks."

Belinda made a face. "Weeks without electric curlers!"

In the store, Steff saw things like toothpaste and cookies and hats.

Belinda held her nose and pointed to a small icebox. On it was a sign, *Fish Bait.* She made her mouth go like a fish.

Steff and Paulie laughed and made their mouths go that way, too.

Near one wall, Steff found mugs decorated with trees. She found plates decorated with trees by another wall.

She told Paulie, "I could really organize this store. These decorated mugs and plates should be in one place."

"Ask the twins before you move stuff."

"I know what! I'll make a list of everything here. An inventory list!"

"Better ask first."

Melinda and Belinda counted money.

Belinda said, "I thought you took . . ."

Melinda said, "No, I thought you took . . ."

"Well, I didn't. . . ."

"Well, I didn't either. . . ."

"Well, it's missing."

The twins saw Steff and Paulie watching. Melinda smiled at them and fluffed her hair. So did Belinda.

Their hair was the color of the red-brown bark on the giant sequoias.

Steff fluffed her hair, too. She kept her arm up so it hid her mouth as she told Paulie, "Something's wrong."

3

the grumlet grumps

Later, Belinda took Steff and Paulie to the crafts cottage.

Tables on the porch were smeared with paint—mostly blue.

Inside, a girl sorted wooden beads. She looked younger than the twins.

Belinda said, "Hi, Judith. I see you taught a blue craft yesterday."

Judith pointed to a tiny wooden wagon. It was painted blue and filled with dried flowers.

Steff asked, "What else do you teach?"

"Oh, a picture frame, a letter holder—stuff like that. Look around."

Paulie liked a cornhusk doll.

Judith said, "I do cornhusk dolls tomorrow morning."

Something fell on the floor.

Quickly, Judith picked it up.

Steff thought it was a key.

Judith kept whatever it was hidden in a tight fist. Except a piece of yarn stuck out.

That afternoon, Steff worked on her inventory list for a while.

Then Chet took her and Paulie to the stable. They waited with other people for the horseback ride to begin.

The trail hands, Ned and Zachery, scowled a lot.

Ned told the riders a hundred times to stay close together.

Steff winked at Paulie. Paulie whispered in Steff's ear, "The Grumlet Grumps!"

The ride finally started.

Steff thought her horse was the nicest horse

she'd ever ridden. His name was Mr. President.

Everybody rode along the dirt road that ran from the stable to the highway. Suddenly, Steff's horse broke away.

Mr. President trotted down an old trail covered with grass and weeds. Long ago, it might have been a logging trail used to carry logs.

"Get back here!" yelled Ned.

Steff tried to stop Mr. President, but he kept going.

Ned caught up. He called Mr. President names that were not nice.

Steff felt as if Ned meant the names for her, too.

Ned jerked Mr. President around and led the horse back to the others.

After the ride, Chet and Steff and Paulie walked away from the stable.

Suddenly, a boy on a bicycle zoomed across the path.

A flash of red glinted in the sun.

A shiver ran down Steff's back. Something about the flash of red made her feel uneasy.

But she didn't know what.

4

flat-face mcgraw

Campfire began at dusk.

Steff and Paulie sat between the twins on benches made of split logs. Tall trees grew all around. A big fire roared.

Mr. Grumlet led songs about belly-elly eels and a bee that lived in a tree with a flea.

Everybody did motions to the songs.

A man wearing black tennis shoes talked about sports and swimming at the resort.

"That's Coach John," said Melinda.

Then came more songs.

The fire burned low. Darkness closed in around the log benches.

Everyone grew quiet.

Mr. Grumlet was not singing funny songs now. He spoke slowly in a deep voice. "A legend has been told in these mountains for as long as anybody can remember. The legend of Flat-Face McGraw."

The twins scooted close to Steff and Paulie.

"Oooh!" Belinda murmured. She put her arm around Steff.

Mr. Grumlet turned his head, as if looking for things in the dark woods.

Steff felt like giggling—sort of.

Mr. Grumlet began.

Many years ago—when there was no Grumlet Giant Trees Resort—Flat-Face McGraw and his gang stole things from the people who lived in the valley below. Again and again, the gang swooped through the valley. They took whatever they wanted. No one could stop the outlaws.

The gang always rode away toward these mountains. Some people thought the gang's hide-

out was close to this very spot. But the hideout was never found.

One night a terrible storm came—worse than any storm before or after. Rivers rose. Lightning flashed.

It is said that one of the biggest and oldest giant sequoia trees fell during the storm—toppled by the wind. Some people think that Flat-Face McGraw met his end at the same moment— squashed beneath that fallen giant sequoia.

Well, the raids in the valley did stop after that. But the valley people couldn't forget Flat-Face McGraw.

And even today, when a wild mountain storm strikes, people often remember the giant tree that fell in that storm, and they whisper the story of Flat-Face McGraw.

When Mr. Grumlet finished, Steff and Belinda were holding hands so hard it hurt.

Paulie had almost crawled into Melinda's lap.

Slowly, people clicked on flashlights and began to leave.

On the way back to the cabin, Steff walked

behind Paulie and the twins.

Her flashlight went out. She stopped and shook it. "What's wrong with this thing?" she grumbled.

Startled, she realized that no one answered. She looked around. She was alone.

She saw lights ahead and walked forward carefully.

She found herself near the storeroom.

Whew! She knew how to get to the cabin from there.

Suddenly, Steff heard a sound that made her duck back in the shadows. It was a bump—perhaps a door closing.

Then someone came walking toward her.

5

pleаse come

A flashlight turned on. The light swung back and forth. It shone down on black tennis shoes.

Those shoes belonged to Coach John!

The light shone on her.

"You're Steff, aren't you? Visiting the twins?"

"Yes." Steff's voice cracked. "The others got ahead of me."

"I'll take you to your cabin," said Coach John. "They will be looking for you."

The next morning, Steff and Belinda walked around the resort. They invited people to church on Sunday at the outdoor theater.

Belinda wore a frilly dress. Her red-brown hair shone in the sun.

Some people talked with her a long time. Some asked questions. She showed them pages in her Bible.

She also told people about the morning Bible study and the Bible story hour.

One lady in a bathrobe started to cry. Her baby was sick.

Belinda yanked a little phone from her bag and called the nurse. Then she held the screaming baby while the woman got dressed.

The baby threw up on Belinda. So she and Steff walked back to the cabin.

Belinda went in the bathroom to take a shower.

Steff picked up a magazine about houses and furniture. A picture inside showed Belinda and Melinda standing in a beautiful house. They had won a prize for decorating it.

Everything in the picture seemed too pretty

to be real. Even the twins.

They looked different from twins who would hold sick babies, and feed boys who couldn't feed themselves, and help people find answers in the Bible, and sell smelly fish bait.

Belinda came out of the bathroom.

Steff asked, "Didn't you feel yucky when that baby threw up on you?"

Belinda wrinkled her nose. "Sure."

"But you kept smiling."

"Hey, I wasn't just smiling at a sick baby. I was smiling at the Lord."

Steff didn't understand. "What you do here at the resort seems so . . . so different than other stuff you do." She pointed to the magazine.

Belinda laughed. "Melinda and I have a special Bible verse. We try to remember it all the time. No matter what we do. No matter where we are. It's Colossians 3:23.

"*Whatever you do, work at it with all your heart, as working for the Lord. . . .*"

Belinda and Steff got to the store at the same time Paulie came in carrying her new cornhusk doll.

Melinda hardly looked at the doll. She told Belinda, "Some money is missing from the store."

"Again?" moaned Belinda. "Mr. Grumlet will think we are terrible store managers."

Melinda's voice wobbled. "So terrible that he might not want us to be store managers anymore."

Steff got an awful feeling. She remembered when her dad lost his job. He had not been a terrible manager. There just wasn't any more work for him to do. And he couldn't find another job. That's why he and Mom had started the family business.

Melinda said, "If Mr. Grumlet doesn't want us to be store managers, we can't stay here."

"That means . . ." Tears filled Belinda's eyes.

"We will lose our Little Ministry in the Big Trees."

6

MYSTERY MAN

Sunday morning, Steff and Paulie and the twins went early to the outdoor theater.

Belinda pulled a cart over the bumpy path. On it was a heavy box of Bibles. Paulie had song sheets. Steff carried Melinda's guitar. Melinda dragged another cart that held a folding table and a broom.

After they swept the log benches, Paulie asked the twins, "Is this work harder than decorating houses?"

Belinda winked. "Yes, but it brings bigger rewards."

Melinda laughed and held out her hands. "Like broken nails."

Pastor Harl had driven up from the valley for the church service.

Lots of people came. Chet was there. So was the boy in the wheelchair.

Melinda played her guitar.

Pastor Harl talked.

When it was over, Steff didn't want to leave. Church outside in the sequoias was special.

Steff opened her Bible to Colossians 3:23 and showed Paulie the twins' Bible verse.

Their parents would have liked church in the sequoias, too. Steff would tell them about it next time they talked on the telephone.

The twins had invited all the children at the resort to meet at the ball field that afternoon.

"We have millions of ways to play games with Bible stories," Melinda told the girls. "Like the Moses relay. And David's toss."

After lunch, they packed up and started for the field.

Steff stopped at a signpost. "Is it okay if I take that trail?" She pointed to a path that went the long way to the ball field.

The twins decided it would be OK.

Paulie said, "Should I come with you?"

Steff shook her head. She knew Paulie was anxious to get to the ball field. Besides, Steff wanted to be by herself for a while.

She walked swiftly, going farther and farther into the woods.

She thought about the twins helping people.

She helped people sometimes. Back home, she was a reading buddy. She helped a boy named Vincent read books.

But Vincent always had sweaty hands. He got the pages wet.

Steff had tried and tried to trade Vincent to another reading buddy. But no one wanted Vincent.

A pain shot through Steff's foot.

"Ouch!"

Her voice sounded loud. She must be miles from everyone.

She took off her shoe and shook out a rock.

Suddenly, harsh words sounded nearby.

They flew through the woods like arrows.

Steff crouched low.

A man was talking. She had heard that voice before. But she didn't know who the man was or what he said.

She tried to tie her shoe. Her fingers shook.

A second person spoke. "One telephone call to certain people . . ."

Steff knew who said that.

It was Coach John. What did he mean?

Now the first person said angrily, "Troopers sometimes get lost up here."

Steff's fingers caught in the shoelace and turned white.

The angry voices stopped.

The soft forest sounds returned. A bird called.

Coach John and the other man—a mystery man—had talked of troopers. How strange.

Did troopers mean the state police?

Who was the mystery man?

Steff crept away. She broke into a run.

She ran all the way to the ball field.

7

Late delivery

At the store the next morning, Melinda waved her key. "Pink opens the door to our store," she sang.

Belinda sang, too. "The camping gear comes toda-a-ay."

The driver who was bringing the shipment telephoned.

"He's on his way," Belinda said.

Then came another call. The driver said he would be late.

Then came another call. The driver would be even later.

At dinnertime, they sighed and closed the store.

Melinda walked backward to the dining hall so she could keep watching for the delivery van.

Belinda carried her little telephone.

The van did not come.

After dinner, they went into the recreation hall. It was movie night, with popcorn.

Mr. Grumlet sat near the twins and Steff and Paulie to watch the movie. Judith sat nearby.

Coach John was not there. He had gone to the valley and would stay all night.

Belinda's phone rang.

She put it to her ear and rushed outside.

Melinda scrambled after her.

Later, the twins returned.

"The shipment is safe in the storeroom," Belinda told Mr. Grumlet in a loud whisper. "The driver was in a big hurry. We made him wait while we counted every box."

When the movie ended, Mr. Grumlet told the twins, "Come on, I want to see this fancy camping gear."

But Judith stopped him. "Mr. Grumlet, a window at the crafts cottage is stuck open."

Mr. Grumlet looked unhappy.

Judith said, "It might rain tonight. Can you come help me?"

Mr. Grumlet looked even more unhappy. But he went with Judith.

Steff and Paulie waited with the twins.

Mr. Grumlet didn't come back.

Paulie yawned.

"I give up," said Melinda. "Let's go to the cabin."

"Okay," said Belinda. "He must be having trouble fixing the window."

The next morning, Mr. Grumlet came to the store.

He told the twins, "Now, let's go to the storeroom and see that camping gear."

A minute later, Steff and Paulie heard a loud scream.

They ran to the back of the store and looked out.

The twins stumbled from the storeroom. Mr. Grumlet followed.

Melinda clapped her hands to her face. "How could it be gone? It was there last night."

"The driver took the boxes from his truck. . . ."

"And put them there!" Melinda pointed inside.

Mr. Grumlet jammed his hat on his head. "You're sure you locked the door?"

"Yes!" said Belinda.

"Of course!" said Melinda.

The twins clung to each other and began to cry.

Mr. Grumlet stomped away. As he went, he said, "I'm calling the sheriff."

Meeting at the big Stump

That afternoon, Steff and Paulie and Chet met at a big stump by the path to the stable.

Chet said, "The sheriff doesn't have any clues about who stole the camping gear."

"How do you know?" demanded Steff.

"Dad sent me to the office. I heard Mr. Grumlet and the sheriff talking. The sheriff said Ned and Zachary spent all night in the valley."

Paulie shrugged. "Guess they didn't do it."

"And the sheriff said that Coach John came

back sometime in the night."

"Hmm," said Steff. "He was supposed to be gone all night."

"Here's something weird," said Chet. "Someone would have needed a truck or a van to carry away that camping gear. No one heard a truck or a van drive out of here in the night."

"Double-hmm," said Steff.

"One more thing," said Chet. "The store-room door was not broken."

"The twins would never leave it unlocked." Paulie looked at Steff. "Would they?"

"Of course not." But Steff was worried. That shipment cost thousands of dollars.

She said, "If Mr. Grumlet thinks the twins are not doing a good job, they will have to leave."

Paulie said, "If they leave, who will tell the people at Grumlet Big Trees Resort about Jesus?"

Steff clenched her fists. "We are going to find the crooks who stole that shipment."

"Yes!" cried Paulie.

"I have an idea," said Chet. "Maybe one

twin lost a key and a crook found it."

"They both had keys this morning," Steff told him. "Silver with pink plastic on the round end."

"Just like a key Judith has," Paulie said.

Steff whirled to her sister. "Say that again."

"Just like a key Judith has. I saw it hanging on yarn around her neck when I was making my cornhusk doll."

Steff snapped her fingers. "Of course! Judith *did* drop something that looked like a key the first time we were in the crafts cottage. She hid it in her hand."

Chet said, "You don't know if that key unlocks the store."

"You're right," said Steff.

But after dinner, Steff told Paulie, "Let's go by the crafts cottage. We might see something."

Steff and Paulie crept to a back window.

Paulie climbed on the roots of a big tree to be taller.

They were still looking inside when Steff heard footsteps. She peeked around the corner of the cottage.

Coach John stood at the front door of the Grumlet Giant Trees Store.

Steff stepped on a dry limb. *CRACK!*

Coach John jumped from the porch. "Who's there?" he demanded.

"It's me, Steff Larson. And Paulie Larson."

"It's time for campfire." His voice was gruff. "Don't dawdle."

Steff and Paulie hurried away.

Steff looked over her shoulder once. Coach John was watching them.

She remembered the angry voices she had heard in the woods. Coach John had said, ... *one telephone call to certain people* ... The other man talked about troopers. Maybe he meant police.

Could Coach John have anything to do with stealing the camping gear?

Had he planned to sneak into the store tonight?

Steff caught her breath.

What if Coach John thought she and Paulie were spying on him?

9

galloping Hooves

The next day, Steff and Paulie stayed far from Coach John.

They went horseback riding in the afternoon.

The riders moved down the dirt road that went from the stable to the highway. Soon Ned would lead everyone onto a riding trail.

Steff wished her mom and dad could see her on Mr. President.

Dust puffed from the road. Wild flowers grew near.

She pretended Ned wasn't around. How great it would be to just ride and ride.

Steff urged Mr. President forward. Little by little, she moved ahead of everyone, even Ned.

She neared the spot where, on another ride, Mr. President had trotted off the road.

Just then, Steff thought she saw a flash of red.

She looked. It was true. Nearly hidden by branches, a bit of red gleamed high on a tree trunk.

Steff didn't take time to think. She pulled the reins. Mr. President turned from the road.

He trotted through the trees along the old trail. Steff urged him on.

Any second, Ned would discover what she had done.

Another bit of red flew by.

From behind came the swift pounding of hooves.

"Whoa!" Steff called. But she left the reins loose.

In a rush of galloping hooves, Ned caught up. He jerked Mr. President to a stop.

"This horse likes to go off by himself," Steff said.

Ned didn't answer. He led Mr. President back to the dirt road and the other riders.

A vein in Ned's neck pumped in and out. It moved faster than Steff's own heart was beating.

Why was Ned so angry about her riding on an old logging trail?

All the riders might have liked seeing what Steff saw there—a pretty clearing where a giant sequoia had fallen many years before.

The trunks of these big trees snapped into huge pieces when they fell. She saw part of one piece. It was as wide as a cabin and longer than a telephone pole. Old, dried roots curled over the end.

Back at the stable, Ned muttered things to Zachery.

Steff was sure he was talking about her.

Ned seemed more and more angry. He spoke louder and louder.

She heard his words clearly.

"Snoopers sometimes get lost up here."

51

Steff had found the mystery man! It was Ned.

In the woods Sunday, she thought the mystery man told Coach John that troopers sometimes get lost up here.

But Ned had not said troopers. He had said *snoopers.*

And now, she was one of those snoopers.

10

inside the dark barn

After dinner, the girls met Chet at the big stump.

Steff said, "I keep thinking about Coach John and Ned talking in the woods on Sunday afternoon."

"They are both doing strange things," said Paulie.

"Well," said Chet, "we could look around the stable."

Steff gulped. "I don't want to mess with Ned—or Zachery."

"They won't be there now."

Paulie warned, "It's almost dark."

Steff gulped again. She clicked her flashlight on and off. Then she jumped up. "We're trying to find the crooks, aren't we? Come on!"

Steff and Paulie and Chet ran to a group of fir trees behind the stable.

Outdoor lights came on around the barn. But it looked pretty dark inside.

"Here's the plan," Steff said. "Paulie, you're the lookout."

"Why do I have to be the lookout? Lookouts have to stay by themselves."

"Would you rather go inside a dark barn?"

"I guess not."

"Okay, then. You're the lookout. You will hide at the front of the barn and warn us if anyone comes."

"How should I warn you?"

"Get a stick and hit the side of the barn two times. Hard. Make it sound as if a horse is kicking."

"Then what?"

"Run around the barn and meet us here at these trees."

"Ready?" asked Chet.

"Let's go," said Steff.

They all raced toward the front of the barn.

Paulie stopped at the door.

Steff and Chet darted inside.

Horses stirred but did not make much noise.

"Don't turn on your flashlight yet," Chet said.

"But this is a barn. We might step in . . ." Steff's toes curled inside her shoes. "Yuck!"

Chet climbed a ladder to the loft.

Steff searched below. She came to a stall with bales of hay stacked high across the front.

Steff squeezed between the bales and the side of the stall. There wasn't room to go far. She stretched out one arm. Her hand touched loose, scratchy hay behind the bales.

Then she felt something smooth.

"Chet," she squealed. "Come here."

Chet climbed on top of the bales and shone his light down.

"What do you see?" Steff demanded.

"A box," he said. "There could be a lot of them."

"The missing shipment!" Steff cried. "Quick, get one."

Chet dropped behind the bales.

Then two things happened at the same time.

Chet cried, "Something's wrong!"

And a sound came from the front of the barn. *WHACK!*

Chet's light clicked off.

Steff held her breath.

WHACK! The sound came again.

"That's Paulie. She's warning us," Steff whispered. "Let's get out of here."

Steff and Chet slipped through the back door.

Outside, they dashed for the fir trees.

They waited and waited.

Where was Paulie?

"Look!" Steff pointed to the barn. "Somebody came out the back door. Paulie was supposed to come from the front."

"That's too big for Paulie," said Chet. "Must be Ned or Zachery."

"He's going into the woods," said Steff. "But here comes Paulie, running like a rocket!"

In the trees, Paulie dropped to the ground. "That was close!"

"Did Ned or Zachery see you?" asked Chet

"No, *they* didn't see me. Ned and Zachery never came."

"What?" cried Steff.

"Another man was sneaking around the barn. He's the one I warned you about."

Steff said, "That must be the man who ran out the back door. Who was it?"

"I don't know. He just showed up."

Steff frowned. "Showed up, huh? Who else always shows up when you don't expect him?"

"Coach John," said Chet.

"Right," said Steff. "Let's not wait another minute. Let's get one box of camping gear."

"Go back to that dark barn?" Paulie's voice quivered.

"Yes. We'll take the box to Mr. Grumlet. We'll tell him everything we know about the trail hands and Coach John. He'll call the sheriff. Right, Chet?"

"Wrong! It won't do any good to go back to the barn."

"Why?" demanded Steff.

"Because," Chet said, "I didn't have time to see if those were camping gear boxes. But I do know there isn't anything in them. The boxes under that hay are empty and folded flat."

"What?" Steff felt like crying.

Finding empty boxes did not solve the mystery of the missing camping gear.

They had not helped the twins at all.

call the Sheriff

The next morning, Steff and Paulie hurried through breakfast.

"We're going to see the horses," Steff told the twins.

Belinda said, "You didn't eat much."

Melinda said, "You girls have been running around a lot. Let's go to the cabin. I'll do your nails. Pearly Pink, I think."

"Petal Pink would be better," said Belinda.

Steff asked, "Can we do our nails later?"

"I suppose," said Melinda.

The twins looked at each other. Steff was sure they were wondering what was going on.

Steff and Paulie met Chet at the fir trees.

Steff said, "Those boxes in the barn must be from the shipment. Why else would they be hidden?"

"But why would the crooks take the camping gear and leave the empty boxes?" asked Chet. "They can sell the stuff for more money if it is packed in its own boxes."

Steff wished she'd thought of that.

"Maybe they'll put it back in the boxes," said Paulie.

"That would mean the camping gear is hidden someplace," said Steff. "And the crooks will come get the boxes."

"Look," said Paulie. "Ned and Zachery are driving away on the hay wagon."

"Good." Steff jumped up. "Let's check the barn again."

Inside the barn, Paulie said, "What a mess. Hay bales everyplace. Where are the boxes?"

"Right where you're standing," said Chet.

"No boxes here."

Chet dug into the loose hay. "They're gone!"

Steff darted outside. The hay wagon was nearly out of sight.

"Ned and Zachery must have the boxes in that wagon," she cried.

Someone came around the corner of the barn. It was Judith.

"What are you guys doing?" she asked.

Surprised, Steff sputtered, "We found the crooks who stole the camping stuff."

"They're getting away!" Paulie pointed down the dirt road.

"That's silly," said Judith.

"No, it's not," said Steff. "That wagon will lead us to where the stolen camping gear is hidden."

Judith's face got red. She waved her arms. "Calm down, kids."

Steff had an idea how to get rid of Judith. "Judith, you go to Mr. Grumlet. Tell him the boxes from the stolen shipment are on that hay wagon. Tell him to call the sheriff."

"I . . . er . . . yeah," Judith said. "I'll take care

of everything. You kids find someplace safe. Stay there."

Paulie tugged on Steff's arm and made a face.

Steff saw why. Coming down the path was someone they did not want to see. Once again, Coach John was showing up at a strange time.

Steff stood on tip-toe close to Judith. She hissed, "Go tell Mr. Grumlet right now. *Run!*"

Coach John came near.

Judith looked unhappy.

Steff glared at her.

Judith turned and left.

Coach John told Steff and Paulie and Chet, "There's no horseback riding now. You shouldn't be hanging around here."

They walked a short way up the path.

Then Steff said, "Let's go back and see what Coach John is doing."

But Coach John was not at the barn.

Steff stared down the dirt road. She couldn't see the wagon. She hoped the sheriff could find it.

A horse neighed. Two boys on bikes

zoomed out of the trees. They skidded in a dusty circle by the barn and rode off.

Steff frowned. There was something about those bikes . . . red . . . the red reflectors on the backs of those bikes!

Steff remembered other bits of red—bright and shiny.

"I've got it!" she yelled. "I know where the stolen camping gear is hidden."

12

the third voice

Steff started down the dirt road. Paulie and Chet followed.

"Steff! Paulie!" someone called.

Steff looked back and waited while Belinda and Melinda caught up.

"Girls, we know you are up to something. Tell us what is going on," said Melinda.

"If you have any ideas about finding bad guys or stolen camping gear," said Belinda, "forget it!"

Melinda shook her finger. "That is not a good game to play."

"We're not playing a game," said Paulie. "Steff knows where the stolen equipment is hidden."

Belinda clapped her hands to her face. "We should call the sheriff. Right now. Oh, I left my telephone . . ."

"In the cabin," said Melinda. "We never have it when we need it."

Belinda raised her eyebrows. "To be correct, we almost never need it up here."

Chet said, "Don't worry. Judith went to tell Mr. Grumlet to call the sheriff."

Steff said, "See the red reflector nailed to that tree? It's like a bike reflector. There are more. They are markers for that trail."

Paulie told her, "That's the trail your horse took."

"Yes. Mr. President had probably been on it before, and I'm sure the hay wagon went that way."

"How will Mr. Grumlet and the sheriff find us?" wailed Paulie.

Steff said, "We need a signal." She looked at Chet. He wore a shirt with a picture of a giant sequoia. "We can hang up your shirt for a signal."

Chet crossed his arms over his chest. "No way."

"Paulie?" Steff began.

"I'm not taking off my shirt!" Paulie shrieked. "You take off something."

"I wasn't going to ask for *your* shirt," Steff told her.

"Oh, okay," Chet said. "Here's mine."

Steff pulled off her belt.

Paulie took off both socks.

Belinda ducked behind a tree. She came back holding her white slip in one hand. She glared at Melinda.

Melinda said, "I don't have a slip or a belt or socks."

Belinda pointed to a long scarf Melinda wore on her head.

Melinda said, "Do you know how much I paid for this scarf?"

Belinda kept glaring.

Melinda sighed and took off the scarf.

When everything was tied together, the signal reached across the dirt road. It flapped in the wind like a clothesline.

"Mr. Grumlet will know we turned here," said Chet.

They followed the trail until they saw the clearing where the giant sequoia lay on its side.

"Stay out of sight," warned Steff.

"Wow!" said Chet. "There's Ned, all right. And there's Zachery carrying a bundle the size of a tent."

Belinda said, "That giant sequoia is hollow, and big enough to walk in."

"They are bringing things out of it," said Melinda.

"*Our* things," said Belinda.

"Yes, our missing camping gear was hidden in a fallen giant sequoia!"

Paulie looked back down the trail. "I wish the sheriff would hurry."

Ned and Zachery took flat boxes from the hay wagon. They folded them back into the shape of boxes. They put the camping gear into the boxes and taped them shut.

Ned peered into the woods on the far side of the clearing. He told Zachery, "The van will be coming from the highway soon."

Steff pointed to where Ned was looking. "There must be an old road over there."

"Yes—a road that only crooks know about," muttered Chet.

The trail hands kept working and talking.

From inside the log came a third voice.

Steff thought Coach John must be inside the log.

But the voice said, "That's the last one, *Dad*."

"Good work," answered Ned.

Someone walked out of the hollow giant sequoia.

It was Judith!

Judith was one of the crooks. She was supposed to be bringing help—bringing Mr. Grumlet and the sheriff. But there she stood, waiting with her father and Zachery for the van to come get the stolen gear.

Steff's knees felt mushy. Her heart pounded.

Judith never meant to go to Mr. Grumlet. Of course not! She was helping her father steal.

The sheriff was not coming!

13

too Late to Hide

Steff tried to sort out what had happened.

She said, "We must get a message to Mr. Grumlet."

Belinda said, "I'll go. People say I run as fast as the wind."

Steff remembered Coach John. No telling where he was. She said, "Take Paulie with you."

"I can't run as fast as the wind," said Paulie.

Melinda said, "I'll bring Paulie."

Steff said, "Chet and I will stay here and stop the van."

"You'll what?" Melinda's eyes flashed.

"I meant, we'll stay here and *watch for* the van."

Melinda grabbed Steff's shoulders. "I won't leave unless you promise to stay out of sight of those awful people."

"I promise."

Steff watched Belinda run down the trail. Melinda and Paulie followed after her. Yes, Belinda did seem to run like the wind.

But that was the way both twins did everything. They worked with all their hearts—just like the Bible verse said—as if they were working for the Lord.

Steff and Chet crept as close to the log as they dared.

The boxes stood packed.

Ned checked his watch and walked to the other side of the clearing.

Chet told Steff, "All I see is brush and weeds under the trees. I can't see any road."

"Maybe the road is marked so the crooks know where it is." Steff gasped and yanked

Chet's arm. "I know! It's marked with red reflectors."

"Just like this trail," said Chet.

"I saw something red on the highway the night we drove to the resort," Steff cried. "It looked like a red eye, but it could have been a reflector. Come on, let's find that road."

They ducked low and ran through the woods.

The van would need to see the markers to find its way from the highway to the clearing.

She and Chet would take down the markers.

They searched for something that looked like a road.

Steff climbed over a rock. She stepped down into a wide path. Weeds grew all over it.

Chet pointed above their heads. A red marker was nailed to a tree.

They had found the old road!

Chet knocked off the reflector with a stick.

He said, "Remember the legend of Flat-Face McGraw and his gang?"

"Sure. He hid in these mountains."

"Some of that story could be true. Maybe Coach John and his crooks got ideas from Flat-Face McGraw."

They hurried along the road. Chet could not get the next marker off. So he covered it with leaves.

Steff found the third marker.

Suddenly, something crashed through brush. It came from the highway. A van!

Steff and Chet dashed off the road.

Over her shoulder, Steff saw the van jerk to a stop.

It was too late to hide.

A man jumped out. He rushed toward them, calling, "Wait!"

"It's Coach John!" Steff yelled. "Run!"

14

Little Ministry in
the big trees

Hands reached for Steff. They caught her. Steff screamed. She tried to wiggle free.

But Coach John held her firmly.

She began to cry.

He said words that didn't make sense.

The next thing Steff knew, Belinda and Melinda were holding her in their arms.

Paulie squeezed in with them. "It's okay, Steff. Coach John is not a crook. He found the boxes in the barn, too. This morning, he saw they were gone, just like we did. He and Mr. Grumlet called the sheriff. Everybody came looking for us."

Belinda said, "They drove along the dirt road until they saw our signal. They turned on the trail and found us."

Chet thumped himself on the bare chest. "Aha! They saw my shirt."

"And my socks!" said Paulie.

"Does anybody have my scarf?" asked Melinda.

"Does anybody have my. . . ?" Belinda stopped. Her cheeks turned pink. She hurried on, "Anyway, Mr. Grumlet and the sheriff and his men are still at the clearing. They have Ned and Zachery and Judith. We heard you and came running."

"The sheriff found out about the old road between here and the highway," Coach John told Steff and Chet. "I drove my van in that way, hoping to find you two. Sorry I frightened you."

"But," Steff said, "we thought . . . you were one of the . . . well, you kept popping up everywhere."

Coach John chuckled. "So did you."

A truck roared up from the clearing. Mr. Grumlet jumped out. "Everybody okay?"

"All okay," Coach John told him.

Mr. Grumlet laughed. "You people gave us a great signal."

Belinda's cheeks turned even pinker.

"I hope my scarf isn't torn," said Melinda.

Steff asked Mr. Grumlet, "Is Judith really a...?"

"Yes, I'm afraid Judith is a thief," said Mr. Grumlet. "We feared Ned was teaching his daughter bad ways, and he was."

Steff remembered Coach John talking to Ned in the woods. He must have been warning Ned about that.

Mr. Grumlet told the twins, "Somehow, Judith had a key to the store and storeroom."

"It was hanging around her neck," said Paulie.

Belinda gasped. "That's why money has been missing from the store."

"And Judith helped steal the camping gear," said Mr. Grumlet. "The delivery man was in on it, too. The police have already caught him."

Coach John said, "Judith told him to bring the shipment during the movie. She hoped everyone would be too busy to open the boxes."

"But on the way, the driver drove to the clearing, where he met Ned and Zachery," said Mr. Grumlet. "They unpacked the equipment and hid it in the giant sequoia log. Then they filled the empty boxes with dirt. The driver brought them to the storeroom."

Belinda said, "We thought we got the real equipment—not boxes of dirt."

Mr. Grumlet said, "Judith saw that I was going to the storeroom after the movie. She didn't want me to check the boxes. So she told me a window was stuck. It was. A piece of wood was jammed in the window frame. I think she put it there."

Coach John said, "Later that night, Judith opened the storeroom. She dumped the dirt. Then she folded the boxes flat and hid them in the hay in the barn."

"That's why the sheriff couldn't solve the mystery," Mr. Grumlet said. "No one blamed the driver because it looked as if he brought the shipment. No one blamed the trail hands because they were gone all night."

Coach John said, "And no one blamed Judith because she couldn't have walked away with all that stuff in the night. And no one heard a van or a truck drive out of the resort."

"But she could—and did—dump the dirt out of the boxes," said Mr. Grumlet.

"And hide them in the barn," said Chet.

Mr. Grumlet took off his hat and fanned himself. "Well, let's get that equipment loaded."

"Yes," Coach John said. "And make a *real* delivery to the storeroom."

"I'll help," said Chet.

Steff and Paulie and the twins walked along the trail.

Steff said, "I'll make a list of that camping gear."

Melinda said, "Maybe if we had asked you to do that the night the shipment came . . ."

"Yes," said Belinda. "That would have ruined things for some nasty people."

She hugged Steff. "I think Melinda and I

should get organized like you."

"Right," said Melinda. "We nearly lost our jobs here—and our Little Ministry in the Big Trees."

Steff said, "It's not a *little* ministry. It's a big ministry."

Paulie spread her arms as wide as she could. "It's a *giant* ministry. It's as giant as a giant sequoia tree with two thousand birthdays."

They all laughed and began to run. Belinda could run like the wind. But she let the others keep up.

Steff didn't think Belinda and Melinda would ever get organized. That was okay. She liked the twins the way they were.

And Steff was going to remember their Bible verse. After all, Steff had a ministry, too. A tiny one named Vincent—Vincent with the sweaty hands. Next time she was his reading buddy, she'd work at it with all her heart. She would look at Vincent, and she would smile at the Lord.

the end